this VeggieTales© gift book belongs to:

_____

_____
from

_____
date

**God Is Bigger!** © 2005 Big Idea, Inc.
**VEGGIETALES**®, character, likenesses and other indicia are trademarks of Big Idea, Inc.
**All rights reserved. Used under license**
**Printed and bound in China**

**Published by Howard Publishing Co., Inc.**
**3117 North 7th Street, West Monroe, Louisiana 71291-2227**
**www.howardpublishing.com**

05   06   07   08   09   10   11   12   13   14        10  9  8  7  6  5  4  3  2  1

**Photography by Chrys Howard and LinDee Loveland © 2005 Howard Publishing Co., Inc.**

**ISBN 1-58229-452-6 (God Is Bigger!)**

**God Is Bigger. Music and lyrics by Phil Vischer and Kurt Heinecke.**
**© 1993 Bob & Larry Publishing (ASCAP)**

# God is Bigger!

written by Phil Vischer
illustrated by Casey Jones and John Trent

Everyone gets a little scared sometimes. When we do, the words of this classic VeggieTales® song remind us we don't need to be afraid, because God is always looking out for us. He is bigger than anything we could be frightened of.

Sing along with the enclosed CD as you read the words and enjoy the pictures that bring this special song to life!

You were lying in your bed.
You were feelin' kind of sleepy.

But you couldn't close your eyes because the room was getting

CREEPY!

Were those **eyeballs** in the **closet?**

Was that **Godzilla** in the **hall?**

There was something

BiG
and
HAiRY

casting shadows

on the wall!

# No!
## You don't need to do anything!

# What?
# Why?
# Because...

So, when I'm lying in my bed
and the furniture
starts creeping...

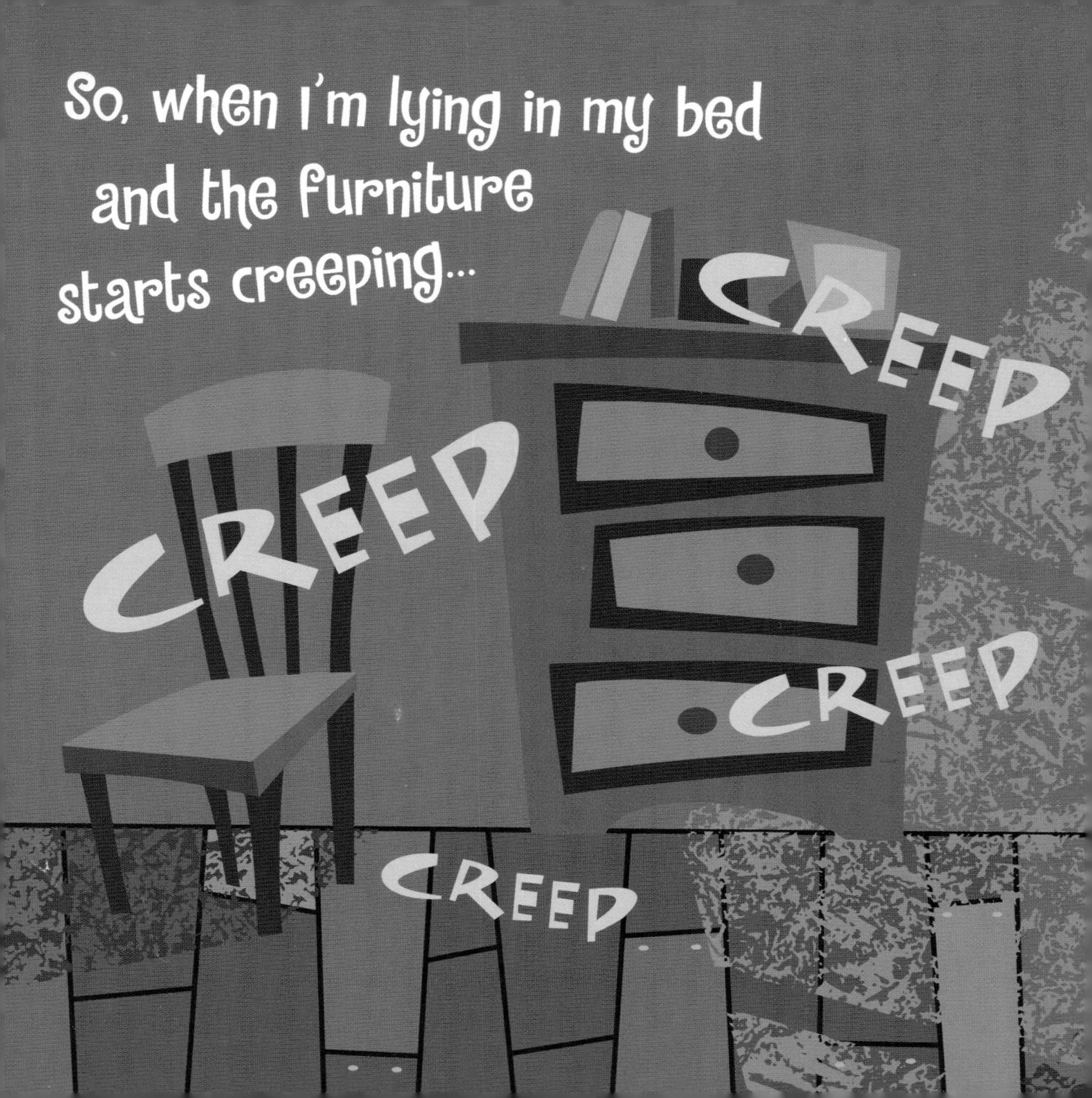

He's bigger than GODZILLA or the monsters on TV.

Oh, God is bigger than the BOOGIE MAN.

And he's watchin' out for YOU and me!

So, are you FRIGHTENED?

No, not really.

Are you WORRIED?

Not a bit.

I know whatever's gonna happen, that God can handle it.

I'm sorry that I SCARED you when you saw me on TV.

Well that's okay, 'Cuz now I know that God is taking care of me!

God is bigger than the boogie man.
He's bigger than GODZILLA
or the monsters
on TV.
Oh, God
is bigger
than the
BOOGIE
MAN.
And he's watchin'
out for you and me!

He's bigger than GODZILLA
or the monsters
on TV.
Oh, God is
bigger
than the
BOOGIE MAN.
And he's watchin'
out for you and me!
He's watchin' out for you and me!

REMEMBER!
God made
you special,
and he
loves you
very
much!

# Collect the entire gift book series! Perfect for any occasion!

Friends come in all shapes and sizes. And sometimes those who could be our best friends are the ones we overlook because we don't accept their differences. *I Can Be Your Friend* colorfully illustrates exactly what it means to be a friend and imparts an important message for children that will last a lifetime.

Based on the best-loved Silly Song with Larry, *Oh, Where Is My Hairbrush?* is sure to delight every VeggieTales® fan. Bright, colorful illustrations, as well as a sing-along CD of "The Hairbrush Song," will make this book a keepsake that your children will always treasure.

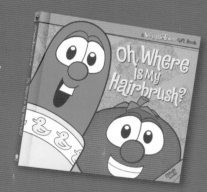

Do you ever wonder why we tell everyone about our day except for the One who is powerful and loving enough to help us through the next one? *My Day*, with its colorful pictures and fun messages, shows children how to develop a relationship with God through prayer.

# CD of accompanying VeggieTales® song included with each book!